ROSIE

The Practically Perfect Puppy

Written by

Beth Schulman

Illustrated by

Sara Farrell

OWL
PUBLISHING

For Ezekiel,
Happy Reading
Sara M Farrell
2019
♡ Beth Schulman
2019

Owl Publishing, LLC.
150 Parkview Heights Road
Ephrata, Pa 17522
717-925-7511
www.OwlPublishingHouse.com

Mrs. Sable and her sons fell in love with the little white puppy
the minute they saw her wagging her stubby tail and poking
her wet nose through the bars of the cage at Petland.

1

"Can we get her, Mom?" James asked.
"Pleeeease," Ian pleaded, putting his face close to the cage. The puppy nibbled his glasses.

"I don't think our apartment is big enough for a dog," Mrs. Sable said.

"But she's so small," Ian said.
"She won't need much room," James said.

"Well, she is awfully cute and she seems friendly." Mrs. Sable stuck her hand through the space between the bars and the little white puppy licked her fingers.

"Will you boys promise to help take care of her? She'll need to be fed twice a day and we'll have to take her for lots of walks. Puppies are full of energy."

"We will, we will," the boys sang in unison.

3

James wanted to name their new puppy Rosalita, but Ian insisted on Lollipop.
"Rosalita Lollipop Sable," Mrs. Sable nodded her head and said,
"That sounds just right. We can call her Rosie for short."

In no time at all, Rosie became a beloved member of the Sable family. Rosie woke James and Ian each morning by jumping on their beds and licking their noses.

"You're our perfect puppy," the boys would say as they gave Rosie her morning hugs.

Rosie, wagging her stubby tail, greeted James and Ian each afternoon at the door when they came home from school.

"There's our perfect puppy," they'd say as they patted her curly head and raced to the kitchen for a snack.

Rosie sat under the Kitchen table while James and Ian did their homework and waited patiently for them to finish.

She guarded the Lego castles they built...

9

...and cheered them on when they played soccer in the hall.

Rosie curled up with the boys while Mrs. Sable read them their bedtime stories and tucked them in.

Mrs. Sable would kiss the boys on the tops of their heads and scoop Rosie up in her arms.

Rosie sat on Mrs. Sable's lap while she drank her cup of tea and watched her favorite show.

"Such a perfect puppy," Mrs. Sable whispered and gave Rosie a rub on her belly.

One day when Mrs. Sable was cleaning the apartment she found a chewed up piece of bubble gum under the coffee table in the living room...

...and another piece on the couch...

...and another behind the TV.

Mrs. Sable was **mad**!

She stomped down the hallway toward James and Ian's bedroom.

Before she reached the door, her foot got stuck to **another** piece of bubble gum.

Now, she was **really** **mad!**

The very next day, Mrs. Sable sat down to read the mail and the last envelope stuck to the kitchen table.

"**Bubble gum**," she grumbled through gritted teeth.

"**You're both grounded!**" Mrs. Sable yelled when James and Ian got home from school. "I found more *bubble gum* on the kitchen table!"

James said, "It wasn't me!"
Ian said, "It wasn't me!"

Mrs. Sable said, "No more lies. **Go to your room!**"

Rosie followed the two miserable boys down the hallway. She sat by their door with her head hung low. Rosie loved James and Ian and when they were sad, she was sad.

Later that week,
Mrs. Sable got home
from work early and
she couldn't
believe
her eyes!

She headed straight to the kitchen and baked a big batch of James and Ian's favorite cookies.

Then, she made a card and placed it next to the warm cookies on the kitchen table.

21

When the boys got home, Mrs. Sable gave them each a big hug and apologized. She took their hands and led them into the kitchen.

Mrs. Sable began, "I'm so sorry I blamed both of you. You'll never believe who I found chewing **bubble gum** on the couch when I came home today."

After a moment's hesitation, the boys looked at each other, smiling, and said, **"Rosie?!"**

Mrs. Sable giggled, "Yes! She had a guilty look in her eyes and a wad of bubble gum in her mouth!"

They all started to laugh.

"I guess Rosie isn't really a perfect puppy after all," said James. Mrs. Sable shrugged, "I suppose no one is **really** perfect." "Well, she's **practically perfect!**" said Ian.

Rosie barked in agreement.

"Be a good girl," Mrs. Sable called to Rosie as she and the boys were leaving the apartment the next morning. She winked at the boys and whispered,

"Don't worry, I got rid of all the **bubble gum**."

For the real Rosie, James and Ian-
all grown up now, but still "practically perfect"
-BS

For Brandi Snifferdog Raysinger,
for seventeen years of licks and laughs
-SF

About the Author and Illustrator

Beth Schulman is a mother, teacher and avid reader and writer. She graduated from The Pennsylvania State University with a Bachelor of Science Degree in Individual and Family Studies and from Cabrini College with a Master of Education Degree, with a focus on Early Childhood Education. She has been teaching elementary school students for over 25 years and is currently a Kindergarten teacher in the Upper Dublin School District. Beth has devoted her life's work to creating supportive, creative and literacy rich learning environments for young children.

Beth lives in Montgomery County, Pennsylvania with her two teenage sons, James and Ian and their dog, Rosie (who is no longer a puppy, but is still "practically perfect").

Beth is also author of, The Gold Mailbox, a memoir.

Sara Farrell is an artist, teacher and long time dog lover. She graduated from The Pennsylvania State University with a Bachelors Degree in art education and a minor in art history. She also received her Masters of Education from Gratz College. Besides illustrating several children's books, Sara is an elementary art teacher and has been colleagues and classroom neighbors with Beth Schulman for over a decade. She loves coming to school each day to share her excitement and passion for the arts with the children in her classes.

Sara currently lives with her husband and young daughter in a suburb of Philadelphia. Along with drawing and painting, she enjoys spending time outdoors with her family and friends.